written by
NYASHA WILLIAMS

illustrated by
JADE ORLANDO

ALLY BABY CAN

BE AN ECO-ACTIVIST

HARPER
An Imprint of HarperCollinsPublishers

Who can be an eco-activist?

ALLY BABY CAN!

Ally Baby makes a change when they lend a hand!

Some things that humans do can cause our planet to hurt.

Eco-activists are allies who stand up for the Earth.

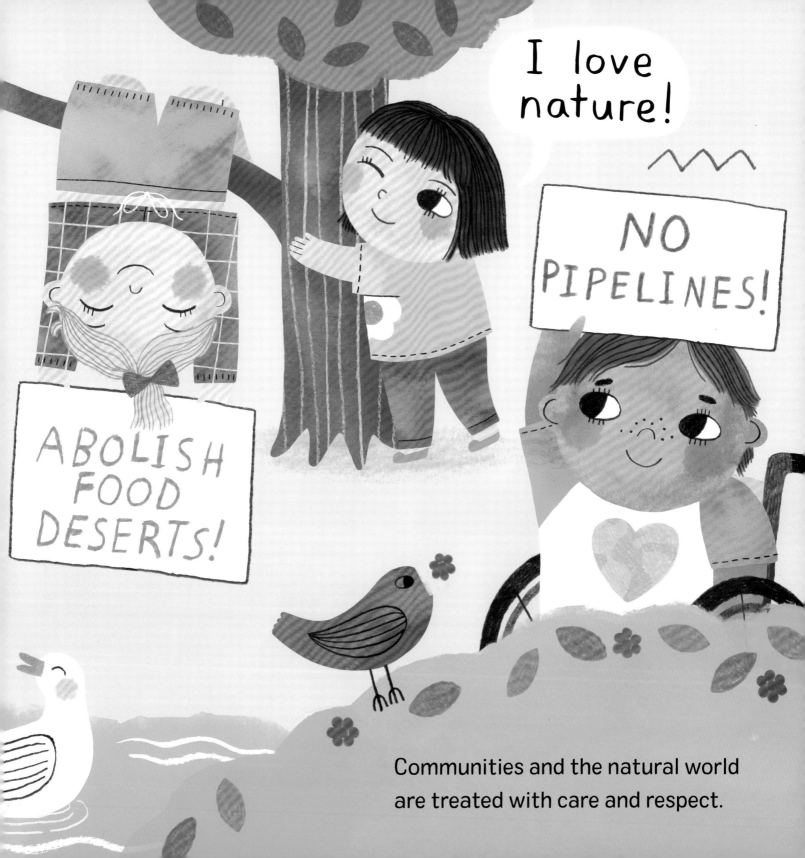

Communities and the natural world
are treated with care and respect.

Ally Baby **COMBATS** resource depletion, pollution, and global warming.

RESOURCE DEPLETION

Human overuse of natural resources, which causes scarcity.

POLLUTION

Human introduction of harmful materials into the environment.

GLOBAL WARMING

An increase in the temperature of Earth's atmosphere caused by human activities, such as pollution and fossil fuel use.

Fighting for environmental justice is Ally Baby's calling!

Ally Baby knows equal access to a healthy Earth is best for you and me.
That's why they **ADD ECO-ACTIVISM** to their everyday routine.

ALLY BABY DOES THIS EVERY DAY

SPEAKS OUT

STANDS UP

PROTECTS

LEARNS

ALLY BABY WAKES UP!

Ally Baby **PLANTS** trees and flowers with Nana in the yard.
Neutralizing carbon emissions can be fun and isn't hard.

Ally Baby works side by side
with generations past.
Ally Baby CREATES a future where
our planet, Earth, will last.

Ally Baby **EATS** a balanced breakfast
full of veggies from outside.

spinach
smoothie

zucchini muffins

carrots

BREAKFAST
TIME!

veggie omelet

oatmeal

Ally Baby learns to reduce their carbon footprint with pride.

PLAYTIME!

Ally Baby **VISITS** a national park
and wildlife sanctuary.

Eco-conscious field trips
make Ally Baby feel merry.

Ally Baby **SHOUTS**, "Water Is Life!"
They **SUPPORT** protectors on the front line.

Ally Baby **PICKS UP LITTER** everywhere.
Rubbish and trash go bye-bye!

AFTERNOON STROLL!

Ally Baby **FINDS** affordable goods
that are regenerative and green.

Ally Baby **VOTES** for sustainable policy that keeps our planet clean.

VOTE

Ally Baby **RIDES** in cities that provide eco-friendly ways to move. Clean transportation and bikeable streets help us use less fossil fuel.

GOING HOME!

Ally Baby **SHOPS** for dinner at the farmers market down the street.

Ally Baby **CHOOSES** cruelty-free items they can compost or reuse on repeat.

Ally Baby **READS** books about the many ways humans need the Earth. Ally Baby **LISTENS** to leaders who put our planet first.

RON FINLEY

GRETA THUNBERG

XIUHTEZCATL MARTINEZ

LADONNA
SANDERS R

BEDTIME!

Ally Baby yawns and stretches
just before they close their eyes.
Ally Baby dreams of a GREENER EARTH
and the day that we all rise!

Ally Baby fully commits to the ally work they do.
Ally Baby CAN be an eco-activist and yes, friends,

SO CAN YOU!

ALLY BABY DOES THIS EVERY DAY

SPEAKS OUT

STANDS UP

PROTECTS

LEARNS

Ally is more than a noun; it is a verb.
As an ally, you can take action to save our planet when you:

ADVOCATE: Use your voice to vote for sustainable policy and to choose lawmakers who prioritize our Earth in balance with human needs.

LEARN: Educate yourself, your family members, and your friends about eco-friendly ways to live and how to make our planet clean and equitable.

LET GO: Challenge your ideas of convenience. What may be convenient for most (like gas-fueled cars or water pipelines) can not only harm our planet but become hazardous to vulnerable communities. When we take care of the Earth, we take care of all life-forms who live on it.

YIELD RESULTS: Take action by decreasing your carbon footprint, shopping locally, reusing dishes, and more!

ALLY BABY . . .

learned about the condition of our planet.

planted new plants and trees in their community.

worked with elders, showing that each generation plays a role in creating a better planet for the next.

bought and ate vegetables grown by local farmers.

visited public spaces that help preserve our planet, such as wildlife sanctuaries, conservatories, and parks.

supported eco-conscious Indigenous communities who are fighting to keep their water and resources unsullied by pipelines and other hazards.

picked up litter.

voted for sustainable policy.

rode bikes, used energy-efficient transportation, and fought for it to be accessible to all people.

used compostable and reusable items.

read books by diverse eco-activists about ways to save our planet.

What is one way you can be Earth's ally today?
How will you advocate, learn, let go, and yield results?

ALLY BABY'S FIRST WORDS

A vocabulary list for Earth's allies:

CARBON FOOTPRINT: the total amount of greenhouse gas emissions that comes from the production, use, and end-of-life of a product or service.

COMPOST: a mixture of plant and food waste and organic materials used to fertilize and improve soil.

CONSERVATION: using resources through protective and regenerative systems, preventing waste or harm of any resources.

CRUELTY-FREE: when a product and its ingredients are not tested on animals.

ECO-ACTIVIST: a person who prevents damage to the environment and communities.

ECO-CONSCIOUS: an effort to live, buy, and consume in ways that are not harmful to the environment.

EMISSIONS: fossil fuels released into the atmosphere (carbon having the highest levels) leading to climate change.

ENVIRONMENTAL INJUSTICE: the damaging health effects of pollution on communities already made vulnerable by marginalization, discrimination, and the imbalance of power.

FARMERS MARKET: a market at which local community members sell homemade foods, fresh produce, and products.

FOOD DESERTS: a community that has limited access to affordable and nutritious food due to an absence of large grocery stores in proximity.

FOSSIL FUELS: fossilized remains of plants and animals that are mined and burned to produce electricity or refined for use as fuel. Coal, oil, and natural gas are common fossil fuels.

GLOBAL WARMING: the global rise in temperatures due to the human creation of greenhouse gases, which trap heat in the atmosphere.

GREEN: a manner or state of being sensitive and less harmful to the environment.

POLLUTION (ALSO LITTER): the process of making land, water, air, or other parts of the environment dirty and unsafe to be used by living beings.

REGENERATIVE: able to regrow, be renewed, or be restored, especially after being damaged or lost.

RESOURCE DEPLETION: the use of a resource faster than it can be replenished. Common resources include water, oil, coal, natural gas, metals, stone, and sand.

SUSTAINABLE: using resources to a level or point where they are not completely depleted.

WATER PROTECTORS: Indigenous and Native activists, organizers, and cultural workers focused on the defense of the world's water and water systems.

ALLY BABY'S READING LIST FOR ECO-ACTIVISM

Dear Earth . . . From Your Friends in Room 5 by Erin Dealey

What's the Commotion in the Ocean? by Nyasha Williams

Little Dandelion Seeds the World by Julia Richardson

Michelle's Garden by Sharee Miller

My Friend Earth by Patricia MacLachlan

This Little Environmentalist by Joan Holub

Rocket Says Clean Up! by Nathan Bryon

We Are Water Protectors by Carole Lindstrom

City Green by DyAnne DiSalvo-Ryan

ABOUT THE CREATORS

Photo by Kimberly Salas

NYASHA WILLIAMS is an author, educator, creator, and activist who works to decolonize literature, minds, and spiritual practices one day at a time. She is the author of the picture books *What's the Commotion in the Ocean?* and *I Affirm Me.* You can visit her at www.nyashawilliams.online.

Photo by Raven Shutley Studios

JADE ORLANDO was born on an army base in North Carolina and grew up in a tiny Michigan town. She is the illustrator of several works for children, including *Hey You!*, *Generation Brave*, and *Who Takes Care of You?* Jade currently lives in Atlanta, GA, with her husband, greyhound, and four cats (including two naked ones!). You can visit her at www.jadefrolics.com.

Ally Baby Can: Be an Eco-Activist · Copyright © 2023 by HarperCollins Publishers · Special thanks to Dr. Na'Taki Osborne Jelks, PhD, MPH. · All rights reserved · Manufactured in Italy · No part of this book may be used or reproduced in any manner whatsoever without written permission except in the case of brief quotations embodied in critical articles and reviews. For information address HarperCollins Children's Books, a division of HarperCollins Publishers, 195 Broadway, New York, NY 10007 · www.harpercollinschildrens.com. ISBN 978-0-06-321456-9 · The artist used watercolor, Adobe Photoshop, and Procreate to create the digital illustrations for this book · Typography by Caitlin Stamper.
22 23 24 25 26 RTLO 10 9 8 7 6 5 4 3 2 1 ❖ First Edition